Rudolph
The Red-Nosed Reindeer

ISBN 0-439-44522-1

12 11 10 9 8 7 6 5 4 3 2 1   3 4 5 6 7/0

Printed in the U.S.A.   24

First Scholastic printing, November 2002

Rudolph

The Red-Nosed Reindeer

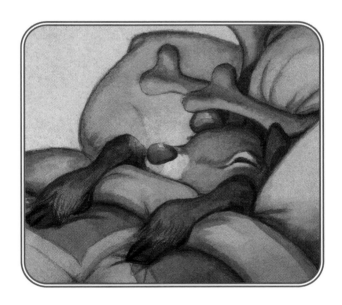

By Robert L. May

Illustrated by
David Wenzel

SCHOLASTIC INC.

New York Toronto London Auckland Sydney
Mexico City New Delhi Hong Kong Buenos Aires

'Twas the day before Christmas, and all through the hills
The reindeer were playing, enjoying their spills.

While every so often they'd stop to call names
At one little deer not allowed in their games.

"Ha ha! Look at Rudolph! His nose is a sight!
It's red as a beet! Twice as big! Twice as bright!"

While Rudolph just cried. What else could he do?
He knew that the things they were saying were true!

Where most reindeer's noses are brownish and tiny,
Poor Rudolph's was red, very large, and quite shiny.

In daylight it sparkled. (The picture shows that!)
At nighttime it glowed, like the eyes of a cat.

Although he was lonesome, he always was good—
Obeying his parents, as good reindeer should!

That's why, on this day, Rudolph almost felt playful.
He hoped that from Santa, soon driving his sleighful

Of presents and candy and dollies and toys
For good little animals, good girls and boys,

He'd get just as much (and this is what pleased him)
As the happier, handsomer reindeer who teased him.

So as night, and a fog, hid the world like a hood,
He went to bed hopeful; he knew he'd been good!

While way, way up North, on this same foggy night,
Old Santa was packing his sleigh for its flight.

"This fog," he called out, "will be hard to get through!"
He shook his round head. And his tummy shook, too!

"Without any stars or a moon as our compass,
This extra-dark night is quite likely to swamp us.

To keep from a smash-up, we'll have to fly slow.
To see where we're going, we'll have to fly low.

We'll steer by the street lamps and houses tonight,
In order to finish before it gets light.

Just think how the boys' and girls' hopes would be shaken
If we didn't reach 'em before they awaken!"

"Come, Dasher! Come, Dancer! Come, Prancer and Vixen!
Come, Comet! Come, Cupid! Come, Donder and Blitzen!

Be quick with your suppers! Get hitched in a hurry!
You, too, will find fog a delay and a worry!"

And Santa was right, as he usually is.
The fog was as thick as a soda's white fizz.

He tangled in treetops again and again,
And barely missed hitting a huge, speeding plane.

Just not-getting-lost needed all Santa's skill—
With street signs and numbers more difficult still.

He still made good speed, with much twisting and turning,
As long as the streetlamps and house lights were burning.

At each house, first checking what people might live there,
He'd quickly pick out the right presents to give there.

"But lights will be out after midnight," he said.
"For even most *parents* have then gone to bed."

Because it might wake them, a match was denied him.
Oh my, how he wished for just *one* star to guide him!

Through dark streets and houses old Santa did poorly.
He now picked the presents more slowly, less surely.

He really was worried! For what would he do,
If folks started waking before he was through?

The night was still foggy, and not at all clear,
When Santa arrived at the home of the deer.

Onto the roof, with the clouds all around it,
He searched for the chimney, and finally found it.

The room he came down in was blacker than ink,
He went for a chair, but it turned out . . . a sink!

The first reindeer bedroom was so very black,
He tripped on the rug, and burst open his pack.

So dark that he had to move close to the bed,
And peek very hard at the sleeping deer's head,

Before he could choose the right kind of toy—
A doll for a girl, or a train for a boy.

But all this took time, and filled Santa with gloom,
While feeling his way toward the next reindeer's room.

The door he'd just opened—when, to his surprise,
A soft-glowing red-colored light met his eyes.

The *lamp* wasn't burning; the light came, instead,
From something that lay at the head of the bed.

And there lay—but wait now—what *would* you suppose?
The glowing, you've guessed it, was *Rudolph's red nose*!

So *this* room was easy! This one little light,
Let Santa pick quickly the gifts that were right.

How happy he was, till he went out the door . . .
The *rest* of the house was as black as before!

So black that it made every step a dark mystery.
And *then*, came the greatest idea in all history!

He went back to Rudolph and started to shake him,
Of course very gently, in order to wake him.

And Rudolph could hardly believe his own eyes!
You just can imagine his joy and surprise

At seeing who stood there, a paw's length away,
And told of the darkness and fog and delay,

And Santa's great worry that children might waken
Before his complete Christmas trip had been taken.

"And you," he told Rudolph, "may yet save the day!
Your bright shining nose, son, can show us the way.

I need you, young fellow, to help me tonight,
To lead all my deer on the rest of our flight."

And Rudolph broke out into such a big grin,
It almost connected his ears and his chin!

He scribbled a note to his folks in a hurry.
"I've gone to help Santa," he wrote. "Do not worry."

Said Santa, "Meet me and my sleigh on the lawn.
You'd stick in the chimney." And flash, he was gone.

So Rudolph pranced out through the door, very gay,
And took his proud place at the head of the sleigh.

The rest of night . . . well, what would you guess?
Old Santa's idea was a brilliant success.

And "brilliant" was almost no word for the way
That Rudolph directed the deer and the sleigh.

In spite of the fog, they flew quickly, and low,
And made such good use of the wonderful glow

That shone out from Rudolph at each intersection
That not even once did they lose their direction!

At all of the houses and streets with a sign on 'em,
The sleigh flew real low, so Rudolph could shine on 'em.

To tell who lived where, and just what to give whom,
They'd stop by each window and peek in the room.

Old Santa knew always which children were good,
And minded their parents, and ate as they should.

So Santa would pick out the gift that was right,
With Rudolph close by, making just enough light.

It all went so fast that before it was day,
The very last present was given away.

The very last stocking was filled to the top,
Just as the sun was preparing to pop!

The sun woke the reindeer in Rudolph's hometown.
They found the short message that he'd written down.

Then gathered outside to await his return.
And were they surprised and excited to learn

That Rudolph, the ugliest deer of them all,
Rudolph the Red-Nosed, bashful and small,

The funny-faced fellow they always called names,
And practically never allowed in their games,

Was now to be envied by all, far and near.
For no greater honor can come to a deer

Than riding with Santa and guiding his sleigh.
The Number One job, on the Number One day!

The sleigh, and its reindeer, soon came into view.
And Rudolph still led them, as downward they flew.

Oh my, was he proud as they came to a landing
Right where his handsomer playmates were standing.

The same deer who used to do nothing but tease him
Would now have done *anything*, only to please him.

They felt even sorrier they had been bad
When Santa said, "Rudolph, I never have had

A deer quite so brave or so brilliant as you
At fighting black fog, and at steering me through.

By *you* last night's journey was actually bossed.
Without you, I'm certain, we'd all have been lost!

I hope you'll continue to keep us from grief,
On future dark trips, as *commander-in-chief!*"

While Rudolph just blushed, from his head to his toes,
Till all of his fur was as red as his nose!

The crowd clapped their paws and then started to screech,
"Hurray for our Rudolph!" and "We want a speech!"

But Rudolph, still bashful, despite being a hero,
Was tired. His sleep on the trip totaled zero.

So that's why his speech was quite short, and not bright,
"Merry Christmas to all, and to all a good night!"

And that's why—whenever it's foggy and gray,
It's Rudolph the Red-Nosed who guides Santa's sleigh.

Be listening, this Christmas, but don't make a peep,
'Cause that late at night children *should* be asleep!

The very first sound that you'll hear on the roof
That is, if there's fog, will be Rudolph's small hoof.

And soon after that, if you're still as a mouse,
You may hear a "swish" as he flies 'round the house,

And shines enough light to give Santa a view
Of you and your room. And when they're all through . . .

You may hear them call, as they drive out of sight,
"Merry Christmas to all, and to all a good night!"